An Evening
at the
HOTEL

Suanne Laqueur

Suanne Laqueur/Cathedral Rock Press
Somers, New York
www.suannelaqueurwrites.com

Publisher's Note: This is a work of fiction. Names, characters, places, and incidents are a product of the author's imagination. Locales and public names are sometimes used for atmospheric purposes. Any resemblance to actual people, living or dead, or to businesses, companies, events, institutions, or locales is completely coincidental.

An Evening at the Hotel/ Suanne Laqueur. — 1st ed.
ISBN: 978-1-7345518-4-6

For everyone

behind a

"Do Not Disturb" sign.

An Evening
at the
HOTEL

The elevator binged sedately. "The cushier the hotel, the more dignified the elevator bell," she said.

He smiled at her but the smile was disconnected from his eyes. He seemed preoccupied as they stood aside to let the elevator occupants come out. He ushered her in and she noticed, as always, that his "ladies first" protocol was accompanied by the beginnings of a gesture, a hastily-checked impulse to touch her shoulder or the small of her back as she went by. Always his quickness to thwart that contact disappointed her. She wanted to feel that little bit of touch, wanted to be the recipient of his spontaneous, protective chivalry.

The doors purred shut. She reached and pressed 9, moved to the back wall. He reached then, and his hand hovered over the number buttons, index finger extended. One beat of silence. Another. His head turned and he looked at her. Nothing playful in his expression, nothing teasing in his finger hovering over the buttons, rather there was something deadly serious, almost dire in his expression and its single, simple question.

The doors had closed and they were rising now. He had the sensation of moving not up but forward, at a clip, afloat on a fast-moving river, heading straight for a precipice. She was looking at him, her eyebrows furrowed. Did she understand him? She must. She always had. The elevator was past the fourth floor, nearing the fifth.

Was he being a fool?

Something in her gaze softened, grew expansive. She stepped forward, reached out and put her hand on his. She folded his index finger back into his palm, brought his hand back to his side with hers in it.

Fifth floor. Their fingers squeezed and as the sixth chime intoned, he brought her hand up to his mouth.

"Are you sure?" he whispered against it.

"Yes," she said, rolling her forehead against

his arm.

His eyes fell closed with relief.

A seventh chime.

Eighth floor.

She closed her eyes against his sleeve. It had happened so simply. In all her imagined scenarios, of all the ways she had contrived them coming together, she had never envisioned him simply *asking*.

The doors opened at the ninth floor. He laid his forearm against them and motioned, as usual, for her to go first. As she passed him, he touched her—put his hand on her head and let it trail down the length of her hair and her back. Her skin shivered with the pleasure, the almost intense relief of it.

His touch.

His touch and his intent.

They walked down the long corridor, dim peachy light layered with oblique flashes from the mirrors on either side. A deep hum resonated from within the belly of the hotel. Do not Disturb signs dangled from doors, shut tight as secrets. In another minute they'd be in her room, undisturbed. They'd be another secret, another cog in the furtive, nighttime machinery of this building.

He felt a sudden, awed love for the bricks and steel and carpet, as if all of it were a revered church and it was his heart tolling like a great bell, slamming against the wall of his chest in hollow, measured thuds.

He put an arm around her, sliding under her hair until the apple of her shoulder was in the palm of his hand. She moved against his side, fitting beneath the drape of his arm.

This ought to have been brand new, yet it felt

purely familiar.

He thought of the years of keeping her at a respectable distance. They rarely touched. There were the odd times she put her cheek against his and kissed the air over his shoulder in hello or goodbye. Once, on an escalator at the train station, she made him laugh—he couldn't remember the joke, but he remembered the laughing—and she rubbed two playful circles on his back as the moving stairs carried them down.

The times they connected physically were few and far between, yet he never doubted that given the opportunity, she would fit to him easily, like a puzzle piece.

The skin of her shoulder was smooth against his palm and he ached to feel all that softness in both his hands. He couldn't wait to be inside all the things he loved about her.

Her fingers were shaking and she dropped her key card twice. He retrieved it both times and finally dealt with the lock himself. A cool rush of air as the door slowly swung back. It was pure darkness within, only a dim sliver of light came from the window, its drapes not fully drawn.

The door clicked shut softly. As he put on the chain, she set down her purse and cardigan. He was muting his phone, then setting it on the bedside table. She took her own phone and brought up one of her playlists, hit the shuffle button, then set it down by his. Their screens went off at the same time, putting the room in darkness again.

They stood, not speaking. Not touching yet. Letting the music wrap around them, letting their eyes adjust, finding one another's face in the dimness.

"Are you nervous?" he asked softly.

"No," she said, nodding her head.
"Me too ..."

Then she moved to him as he stepped to her and their mouths met with one huge, shared inhale. For a moment they were still, holding each other's heads, holding each other's breath, then she sighed in the back of her throat and he sighed deep in his chest and each exhaled into the other.

Her hands peeled his jacket down his back and off his elbows. He slithered free and her arms reached up around his neck. His wrapped around her waist and he picked her up, caught her up tight, hugged her body full against him. She was small in his arms, but brashly present, clutching him with lean, hard curves.

Her body. Her skin. Her hair. All of it here, now, for him. Nose in the arc of her neck, he pulled in her scent. That orange-y perfume he'd known for ...

Years. I've dreamed of you holding me for years.

His hug was enormous, his arms swallowed her up. He turned around with her once, twice, and she buried her face in his big shoulder and clung to him. Two quick steps and he had her up against the wall by the window and then he took her head, put his hands on her face, his thumbs running along her cheekbones, his forehead to hers. No end of things she wanted to tell him but at that moment she could only say his name, breathe it once just before he kissed her.

God, his mouth on hers.

She was nothing but air and stomach and an enormous, pounding heart. She shivered beneath ...

That grey wool dress he liked so much, a sheath so perfectly tailored it hurt to look at her.

"That's not a dress, that's an Audrey Hepburn movie," one of the managers said once, when she walked into the Monday meeting wearing it with pearls. Slender as a blade, something out of the 1940s.

He glowered inwardly at the remark, wishing he'd made it himself. Perplexed by sudden, petulant jealousy at the smile she beamed in reply.

It was no secret she was his treasured colleague. He took a certain pride in her being well-liked and indispensable to his entire organization. Yet the compliment about her dress annoyed him. It made him realize his pride in her had morphed into something personal, almost possessive. He liked to think she came to see *him* on Mondays and dressed accordingly. For him.

Now he was turning her away from him, to face the heavy drapes at the window of a dark hotel room. Now his hand pushed aside her hair and picked out the tab of the long zipper on that Audrey Hepburn of a dress. This was now, and this was the dress he liked on her but it was coming off. *Now ...*

He unzipped her.

Now I'm undone, she thought.

He held her hand as she stepped out of the circle of the fallen dress, stepped out of each pump, the red ones with the silver buckles. Rarely did he remark on her clothes or appearance but the first time she wore these shoes to the office, with a white blouse and a grey pencil skirt, she got an unchecked comment from him.

"Those shoes make you look—" He stopped abruptly even as his eyes continued to sweep her from head to toe, and he finished with a slightly confused, "Tall."

She loved it. She knew she had his full respect on a business level, but when he noticed her as a woman, it delighted her, as did the charming bit of mental juggling as he'd tried to reconcile both things. Besides, she was tall, taller than most men in the office. His height appealed to her: in heels she could look him in the eye.

Now, having stepped from her we're-not-in-Kansas-anymore red shoes, the crown of her head merely skimmed his chin. His hands were between her shoulder blades again, unhooking her bra—a frisson of regret that she wasn't wearing a nicer one, but how in hell could she have known?

She leaned back against his chest as he slid the straps down her arms. For one gorgeous moment, his arms folded around her from behind, and she was completely naked in his still-clothed embrace. He held her tight, and they were quiet, looking through the gap in the drapes, out the window at the slice of lights across the Hudson, his mouth rubbing against her hair.

Her hands hooked around one of his forearms and she lay her cheek against his sleeve and the edges of the room blurred hot and wet.

They were quiet, yet they were both pulling in deep, labored breaths. The air was so thick and chemical it was impossible to get a lungful. He could feel minute twitches beneath her skin and he made his hold heavier, his hands soothing. He was nervous but not anxious. Calm as he could possibly be with any undressed woman in his arms, but having a slight heart attack at it being her in the altogether, closed up in his jubilant grip. He could barely wrap his mind around having spontaneously and miraculously orchestrated this with merely a look. Yet under the thrilling disbelief was a composed conviction he was meant to be here.

He deserved this.

She sighed in his arms. He wasn't entirely sure what she was feeling but he wanted all or nothing. He didn't want to belabor the point, but she was shaking now, and so was he.

"Are you all right?" he said.

She wasn't sure what she was. Wildly excited, crazed with wanting him, fighting an anticipatory impatience to feel him already. To cut to the fucking chase and pull him down on the bed, even the floor. Pull him on her and make love, feel the long length of him along her body, feel his weight crushing her, feel him inside her.

Yet she didn't want to move from his arms. Not yet. Her heart splashed in her chest and a funny tightness in her throat threatened sobs. Not from sadness. Or fear.

"I'm all right," she said, "I'm just emotional."

There was no point pretending she wasn't caught up in her feels. They'd known each other too long. What would be the point of artifice anyway? Seduction? Getting laid? That had never been her intent. She always knew what she felt for him could never be dismissed as cheap thrills.

They were attractive people—either one of them could stand in a bar and get digits. But instead they were standing here, together by the window, trying to breathe a way into this. He was here. He'd asked to be here. The way he was trembling let her know that this wasn't a conquest. The way he was holding her left no doubt he would move in her like he was born to.

He held her carefully, filled with his own emotions and filling up his eyes from this unusually wonderful vantage point. Standing behind her and looking over her shoulder, down the full length of her body, the view was spectacular. She was a long drink of water. His shaking hands began to wander, sliding down her sides, into the curve of her waist and out the curve of her hips. They traveled up again, enfolded her once more.

"I don't want you to be afraid to tell me you've changed your mind," he whispered, rocking her gently against his chest.

Her head swiveled and she looked up at him. Even in the dim light from the window, he could see the edges of her eyes were liquid, but her face was filled with that signature irony he adored.

"I've changed my mind, please leave," she

said, deadpan.

And forever, the rest of his life, he would have that moment, freeze-framed in a slice of city light, when she was looking up at him, wearing nothing but her skin, with damp eyes and that tongue-in-cheek expression. And he looked down at her, transfixed and smitten, mirroring it all back.

He put his hand on the side of her neck, moved it into her hair, holding her eyes. Growing hard as he felt desire ripple over her skin. Growing harder as they kissed, hungry, then hungrier, then starved. He felt her shiver and turn and spiral into him and they were ...

... backed up against the wall again, out of her heels, out of her clothes, nearly out of her mind. Tucked in the crooks of his elbows, her own arms wound up around his neck as they kissed. Under her hands she could feel all the layers, all the edges and seams of him: where his shirt was still starchy and where it had broken down into softness. The different texture of his tie against her chest. The cool smoothness of buttons and cufflinks on her skin. His belt buckle in her belly and beyond that, him. Hard like iron. Wanting her, wanting her bad, wanting her in the worst way.

Awareness swirled around her head like a sandstorm, shifting waves of dream and reality. It didn't seem possible she was caught up, finally, in his arms. That he was, finally, kissing her, touching her, pulling her against him. This was the feel of his hands, finally. This was the taste of his mouth, at last. This was him, hard for her. He said her name, murmured it like a prayer into her neck. She'd always loved her name in his voice but now his voice was a keen whisper with barely any breath in it. She could feel him trembling, for her. Feel the heat coming through his clothes like a fever, for her.

Her own shaking, hungry hands slid from his shoulders and joined to start loosening his tie. The tie he picked out and knotted that morning, unaware of what the day was going to bring. Never dreaming it would be her deft fingers undoing him.

Not long ago, she told him, as if commenting on the weather: "My passionate devotion to you professionally isn't without passionate curiosity about you as a man."

That passionate curiosity was letting nothing escape her tonight. She took him to pieces, every bit of software and hardware stripped off him as if she were a competent car thief, undressing him like some sublime act of deconstruction. Tie slid from the channel of his collar, his collar stays slid from their secret slots. His watch released, his cufflinks unhinged, his belt drawn from its loops. Everything held momentarily in her wondering, feverish hands, then dropped to the floor and she was moving on again, exploring something new to take apart.

His buttons lovingly undone, shirt tails pulled from his waist and her hands worming between like parting curtains, sliding around his back, pressing up against him. Her bare body like a length of silk through his fingers. Naked, kissing again, she was all up in him, giving him her tongue, her breath in his lungs, following as he walked backward in the dark, pulling her to where the smooth expanse of the bed yawned, beckoning like a giant hand for them to fall into its palm.

The back of his leg hit the box spring and he let go, a magnificent swoon backward with her caught up tight in his arms. A moment's crushing weight on top of his chest before he rolled her down beneath him, ripping up spread and blankets, shedding off the last bits of clothes, the last shreds of reserve.

And then they were in bed, naked and tangled, and he had nothing more to hide behind, nothing left to stop him from assuaging her passionate curiosity and showing her the man he was.

He burst into her like a sunrise, like a ten-fingered chord on the piano, slid straight into her (*Like he was born to*, she thought), hot, golden and syrupy, and she thought she would fly apart at her joints, splash in puddles of joy on the walls.

He made some indescribable sound, and she made yet another. For ten seconds all was madness: they grappled wildly, twisted, writhed, trying to kiss, trying to breathe, trying to be everything. And then he stopped, his hands took hold of her, pressed her against the mattress until the universe came to a slow halt.

"Shh," he said. "Wait a minute."

He lay still within her, hard and huge, filling her up to her eyes. Up on his elbows like a cobra, cradled in her thighs, he held his forehead to hers.

"Are you all right?" she whispered, running her palm along his jaw. He nodded but didn't say anything, didn't open his eyes, and she understood: this hadn't been the plunge, not yet. He was still poised at some final edge.

She knew him then. Knew that beneath his desire to do right by her was a fierce and sometimes uncontrollable passion, and he was about to unleash it on her. He, who had never touched or treated her with anything but cordial respect, was about to hold her down and fuck the top of her head out into space, or scoop her up and love her with glorious tenderness, or both—quite possibly all those things at the same time. His sexuality was going to be so intense, so all-consuming and reckless, so multi-faceted, it would be impossible for him to be inside her without losing himself.

She knew he wanted to be all things to her, and he wanted all of her selves with him, or else none. Anything in between simply would not work. He was trusting her. He could not jump halfway.

"God," he sighed. "You feel ... I'm so ..."

No words in the world could finish that thought. He was in it now. Here she was. For years quietly at his side, discreetly behind the scenes. Not always visible but forever present in a thousand small ways that sweetly oiled the wheels of his job. They'd always marched in step. Not co-workers, they joked, but dance partners. And now, here, undeniably here, this tiny dancer underneath him, face to face, soft hair, sugar and oranges, her lithe body hungry and open and completely attuned to his. Everything she'd always been to him, but now in the dark.

It was still the dance, only turned horizontally.

He tried again. "This is ..."

Once again he failed to find any words for it.

He was *inside* her.

She brushed a finger across his lips, then

kissed him, deep, slow and perfect.

"I know," she whispered.

He looked down at her, looked in her open, confidently adoring eyes. She was in it, too, she was with him, and she knew. He grabbed her hands, grabbed her mouth in his kiss and jumped.

In the days that followed, she could not reconstruct that night with him as a linear event. She could only island-hop from one pleasurable highlight to the next, out of order and overlapping.

He rolled down onto his back, pulling her with him, up and onto him in a cartwheel of arms and legs and a seamless, unbroken kiss. His hands came up, brushing the hair back from her face, then burying his fingers at the back of her head.

He was good. *Fuck*, he was so good. He moved like quicksilver from tender to fierce and back again, weaving together his strength with his sweetness, power with vulnerability, passion with skill. Holding her so hard, kissing her so softly, loving to kiss, he kissed like a dream.

Knees hugging his sides, she had him deep in

her and she couldn't tell where she stopped and he began. And then he said ...

"Christ," he whispered hoarsely.

The air roaring in his head, eardrums bulging against the dark, firework flashes of yellow and orange behind his closed eyelids, her scent dancing up his nose and teasing the back of his throat. The taste of her mouth in his, and through it all he was sliding and pushing inside her and she was sliding and pulling him in. She was beyond belief. No sooner was a desire in his head—for her to go faster, go slower, come down and cover him, or sit up so he could see her—than she was right there. Right time, right place, as if she'd been made for no other purpose than to be his lover.

She was onto him and all over him and she was so damn good at him. God, he could writhe here forever, just being gripped from within and without by her body on top of his, firm flesh and soft skin, shifting muscle and bone, so small but so strong and coaxing from him words he didn't even know he had.

"Christ," he whispered as he gasped out of their kiss, holding her head, holding her mouth still against his, fighting for breath. "Christ, you are so fucking tight ..."

... In the days after, the weeks and months, all it took to make her eyes close with wet, weak-kneed recall, was that single word, in any context:

Tight.

... (*Tight*) ...

Then he sat up, locked his arms around her waist and rolled her again. Now she was down in the tangle of sheets and blankets and he was rising up and over her. The light from the window glinting on his bare back and shoulder and pooling in the hollow of his collarbone. He was silvery and magnificent and completely undone, his hungry mouth against her skin, his hair sliding over his forehead, and it was how she'd longed to behold him—no longer groomed, combed, shirted-and-tied and formal, but on his knees, messed up and fierce and ardent and intent on being her lover. There was an edge to him she'd never seen before, and yet she didn't fear his passion for she felt, deep beneath it, his inherent gentleness, and deeper than that, the weighted history of their years, their instinctive understanding of each other, her devotion to him and his implicit trust in her.

She slid her leg up and around his body, drawing him further down into her.

In his own aftermath, it seemed there was a bullet of memory lodged in his brain. A golden capsule containing the single sensation of her leg, and how the secret skin behind her knee felt as her leg had arced up and around his side. The warm, smooth weight of her calf in the small of his back, followed by its pull. She *dragged* him down into her heat.

He could still feel it. Still hear what she said before her leg had moved like that:

"You feel so good in me."

Then she hooked him, pulled him deeper into her, and with her calf hugging his back she ran her mouth up his neck and whispered, "I knew you would ..."

She knew he would. She'd always known he would be sensational in the dark. His prowess was no surprise, neither was their sexual affinity together. Still, his utter inhibition had some legitimate shock value, for this was one of the most guarded men she knew.

He was neither cagey nor unapproachable, but what was given forth he chose to give forth, and what was kept behind was sacrosanct. There was no swaying him to give up what he didn't want to.

Over the years, he'd only spoon-fed her details of his private life. Despite their easy rapport, even with all the playful and thrilling banter lately, most of his true feelings remained beyond her grasp. She couldn't quite tell if he was intrigued by her, or just mildly amused. Did her attentions please him, or was he used to fawning female company, and so was ambivalent to hers? Did he count her among his blessings or among his worries? Did he ever take her out of the context of their work relationship, or did he just take her for granted as both a co-worker and a woman?

Why tonight? she wondered. *What changed? What made it happen?*

At the client dinner and the crush afterward at the bar, they'd barely interacted. Their glances met a few times, and each time his sweet smile unfolded for her. She smiled back, noticing their eye contact always seemed to go beyond superficial. Still, nothing was remotely flirtatious or sexual about the smiles and glances. No hint he was pursuing her or she him. No definitive moment of "It's on." Nothing more than her telepathic *Sir* across a crowded room, and his returned *Ma'am*.

Walking through the lobby at the same time to meet at the elevator bank had been pure coincidence. And now he was in her room, in her bed. In her body. Looking at the world through her eyes and for tonight, for these precious hours, he belonged to her.

She knew it would be sensational, but had no idea it could be so incredibly soulful.

They lay facing each other in the tangled nest of sheets. She'd moved her leg over his but otherwise stayed very still, eyes closed, expression unreadable.

Her silence didn't bother him. In fact, she was one of the few people with whom he could sit in silence and be perfectly comfortable. She often sat that way on the other side of his desk—present, slightly aloof, quiet, but in a manner that was companionable, not exclusionary. She was a cat dozing on his hearth. Not apathetic to him, but content with what he was and what he was giving.

He enjoyed having her sit with him very much.

I like her company, he always thought when she left his office and the room seemed dimmer.

Once he'd been on the train home, about to doze off, when the image of her sitting with him leaped unexpectedly in his head. For an incredulous moment, she was there, in the seat beside him, dozing as well, her lolling head falling onto his shoulder.

The fantasy appealed to him. He almost told her about it but, as was with so many of his deepest thoughts, he couldn't find the words. Words were her forte, not his.

She lay with him now, his quiet and clever friend, wearing that slightly feline and, to his rather pleased ego, totally satisfied expression. She was lovely. Lovely and wild.

Soon her stillness undid him, and he ran a fingertip down the bridge of her nose, across her lips and off her chin.

"Are you sleeping?" he whispered.

Her mouth curved up but her eyes stayed closed. She shook her head. She took his hand, pressed it flat to her chest and then slid it down her body, due south, moving her leg further up his hip. His fingers found her, found she was wet as all hell, still wide open, still wanting.

"Do that again," she murmured from behind her closed eyelids, her hips pushing toward him, her hand on his.

"Show me," he said.

She said, "Like this."

"Here?" His fingers were long and warm.

"Yes, like ... Slow ... Like that. There. Just like that."

The words fell apart in her mouth, and he hardly needed her direction anyway. He had it. Perfect.

"How old were you when you let a boy do this to you?" he said. His fingers slid deeper in her and his mouth ran hot over her breasts.

The question made her blush with vivid memory, recalling nights with her high school boyfriend: the exploration, the mixture of excitement and trepidation, the frustration of wanting, the frustration of not knowing what she wanted. Arching her breasts to his mouth, pulling her own shirt off. Not skittering away, *no*, from

43

the hand undoing her jeans but pushing her hips toward it, *yes, yes.* And that astounding, pivotal moment when the idea of having a boy inside her, which had always seemed somewhat revolting, suddenly seemed conceivable. More than that, it was astonishingly and achingly desirable. How old had she been on those feverish, experimental nights?

"Seventeen," she said.

He made a small sound of surprise against her collarbone. "And when did you go all the way?"

"Eighteen."

"What a good girl."

She laughed. "It was a school night. A Tuesday, I think. Next day my French teacher said to me, 'You look different today.' I almost died."

His smiled flashed in the dark. "That's hilarious." His hand came sliding up her belly. "I don't know why, but thinking about being in the back seat of a car with you is really hot." His wet fingers brushed her chin. She opened her mouth for them, tasted herself, let them go slowly.

She thought about herself at seventeen, alone with a younger version of him in the hot, steamy cocoon of a car. Windows fogged up and radio running the battery down. Letting him unhook her, unzip her, feel and touch her. She took his hand and pushed it down again.

"Show me what you'd do," she said.

"No, I think we should wait," he replied softly. She swatted his head and he laughed in the dark. She'd heard him laugh more times in the past few hours than in all the time she'd known him. It was wonderful.

"Baby, please," she said, playing along. "Please, I want it so bad."

She took his head and gently closed her teeth around his bottom lip, not wanting any more words or games, just wanting herself and his touch.

They kissed and he touched her, up to his knuckles in her velvet depths. His mind was still fluctuating between their high school scenario and the forty-something reality. Thinking about girls, thinking about women, finally coming back to here and now and her. Here and now was where he wanted to be, and her writhing under his touch was something he'd always wanted to see.

She wasn't a conventionally beautiful woman, but her confidence, her talents, her wit, her ironic humor—often aimed at herself ... All that combined with her looks had taken him slightly hostage, left him reeling in a helpless fascination. What did a woman as self-assured as that look like vulnerable? How would she sound in the throes, exactly how would her head twist into the pillow as you brought her around? These were among his own private wonderings, his own passionate curiosity.

What do you look like when you come?

How could I make you come?

What do you want me to do, tell me what you want, show me, say everything.

He'd always envisioned her being very explicit with him, but the reality was much different: she was telling him all right, but without saying much at all. He was struck by how little difference there was between how they worked together and how they made love. He was in charge, but she was the one behind the scenes, invisibly and wordlessly leading him where he needed to go.

She was leading him to that place now, going deep within, not so much kissing him anymore as simply breathing through his mouth. And with the burning fury of eighteen, he was pushing aside the covers, pushing into her body, blind with the want and need to follow her.

"Wait for me," he whispered.

"You're so good," she said.

They were in the dim, magic hours of midnight now, taking their time. She was loving being on top of him, her belly filled with her man.

"I'm not doing a thing," he drawled indolently.

He had his arms up, fingers interlaced with hers, letting her lean all her weight into him as her hips found a groove, the most perfect, languid rhythm, catching the sweet spot.

Time stretched out like taffy. She became aware of the song coming from her phone's speaker. And wasn't that funny: she, usually so attuned to music, with a host of songs she associated with him in particular, couldn't recall anything that had been playing this whole time. Only now she registered Joan Osborne's smoky voice singing "Little Wild One."

How many times had she walked down Park Avenue, away from the office, away from him, listening to this album—Joan's love letter to New York City. It was the soundtrack to her mental affair with him, the key to how she would invite him into it, if only she knew he wanted to come:

Let's make it simple, just for fun ... Don't speak of this to anyone ...

All the while making love, the sound of her two silver bangles, sliding up and down her forearm, was a funny little xylophone accompaniment. A symphony of tiny clings and clangs every time she moved on him or under him. Whenever she brushed her hair back, when she reached up and around his neck. Up and down her arm, jingling like wind chimes in a summer breeze.

(*I've seen the way you look in my eyes, I know
that you're ready to fly*) ...

Later on they were making love with her in his lap, in the wingback chair. Her long thighs closed him in like a second pair of armrests. She had her hands interlaced at the back of her neck, head lolling and eyes closed as she lazily rocked on him.

He asked, "Is this Heaven?"

She smiled, eyes still closed, pulling all her hair up high on her head and letting it fall again as she answered, "Hell."

Laughing, his hands moved in slow circles around her small breasts, down her sides, caressing the long, lean planes of her legs, the pretty cuts and curves of her shoulders.

"Total hell," she said, with a catch in her voice he was starting to recognize. He was beginning to know her, know her looks and sounds, feel the change in her body's rhythm as she started to go somewhere. She moved more intently now, rising up along the full length of him, tilting her hips just so and driving down into his lap.

"I love making love with you," he whispered.

The quicksand of desire was closing over his head, pulling him down. Her breath was catching in her throat. Her hands had come undone and were drooped by her collarbones, fingers folding down into fists and then curling out again, holding onto the air. He caught them in his.

"Come for me," he said. "Let me see it."

She drew his hands down, pressing them to her spine.

"Scratch my back," she said.

It was easy to tell him secret things. Privileged, sexual things. Only the smallest flicker of shyness as she asked him, "Scratch my back," and the hope he wouldn't question her.

He didn't. He only said, "Like this?" As he did to nearly everything she'd shown him, so curious and willing.

"Like this?" he said, scratching the small of her back and the curve of her waist.

She moved his fingers down to the flat plane of her sacrum. "Here," she said. "Not hard. Just ..."

And then he got it. He had it perfect, his short nails drawing across the small of her back and around the first bump of her tailbone. Triggering that wonderful whatever-the-hell-it-was that felt so damn good. She rocked down on him again, felt him grow harder and more excited by pleasing her, from far away a dire groan from him.

"God, you're going to make me come."

She pulled him up into her as her belly contracted down, like a flower closing up petal by petal. He cried out into her chest as her back opened up to the room under his fingertips.

He had her.

He just *got* her.

"I love your body," he said, even as a magnificent yawn threatened his jaw. He lay on his stomach, in a state of spent, unhinged bliss, one arm around a pillow, the other palm running circles around her butt.

"I can't keep my hands off your ass," he sighed.

A contented hum in her throat. "I pegged you as an ass man a long time ago. Remember?"

He wished he could. When did a teasing familiarity begin seeping into their exchanges? When did she start firing those small, intriguing shots over his bow? How long had she been slowly weaving a web around him before he realized the special attention she paid him was only a small part of an incredibly larger picture?

She's flirting with me, he thought. But that was dissatisfying, not to mention inaccurate. First of all, she flirted with everyone—men and women, old and young. Second, flirting was too shallow a concept. What she did to him was something much more complex. She'd been *watching* him. For years, apparently. Not only watching, but cataloging all their little moments in her prodigious memory.

His own analyst, analyzing him.

Her capacity for total recall was astounding, surpassed only by her ability to make a moment into a story. What he could vaguely recall as an ordinary, everyday interaction, she memorized, applied a little poetic license, embroidered it, took it in here, let it out there, and gave it back to him as a breathtaking, perfectly-captured vignette. It redefined attentive.

It redefined *everything*.

Never in his life had a woman seduced him so cerebrally. She hadn't burst through his front door and blatantly come on to him with an offer of physical delights. She slipped in a side entrance of his brain and waited quietly on the other side of his desk. Won him with wit and words and in return, offered precisely nothing but this ongoing, affectionate attention.

Never in his life, never had there been anything like this.

He ran his hand up her body, weak with

wanting it. Beneath her hair, he caressed the shape of her head, wanting what was in there just as badly. He wanted to talk to her about everything, but the yawns were breaking through. Lying here was too wonderful, luxuriating under the hand caressing him so expertly, rubbing his head and neck and shoulders. Her touch was gorgeous. He wanted to tell her how insanely lovely she was, he had a thousand questions to ask her.

Talk to me, tell me things, he thought, even as the edge of his awareness was beginning to unravel.

She watched him sleep, her fingernail lightly tracing the edge of his sideburn. The neat line at the top of his ear she'd studied so intently for so many years, wondering what it would be like to kiss him there.

She kissed him there now, softly. He made a small sound in his chest, moved further into the ring of her arms, and then was still again. She ran her hand along his neck, a curve she'd often imagined beneath collar and tie. Her hand moved softly down the arm that lay heavy across her body. Often he would come over to her cubicle to talk, standing in the adjacent cube with his arms crossed on the low wall between them. She could discreetly take note of which shirt he'd donned that day, which tie, which cufflinks. Happily admire the little bit of skin showing between his cuff and the button on his sleeve.

Sometimes, she mused he did this on purpose, that he knew damn well she liked him and under the pretense of conversation, he came over to her cube to be checked out.

On a deeper, wiser level she sensed he liked her, liked her attentions, perhaps liked them a little too much, and out of his own deeper wisdom, he always kept something between them—a wall, a desk, a conference table, four feet of space.

Now his body lay full against hers and he was sleeping. And she could look at him all she wanted to. Other than random, pleasurable observations, her head was peacefully empty. She felt no need to deconstruct this. She just wanted to collect it, remember it all, every word, every touch. Never did she think it would happen, yet here he lay, exhaling softly onto her skin, the edges of his hairline damp with sweat.

She stroked his head, and lay awake beside him a long time.

sometimes that Monday Parting Shot didn't come and he'd be bewildered at the disappointment. Yet more often than not, her shots came at a better time: she had an uncanny, almost telepathic ability to text him at the nadir of a crappy day, and if not turn him around, at least make him smile. She knew how and when to reach him. Some days she flat-out saved his ass.

Now, lying in bed with her, he touched the scar on her neck and wondered, being indulgently maudlin, how both his professional and personal life might've been different if she hadn't survived.

Nice, he chided himself. He brushed away the useless drama and he decided to wake her up instead, because she was here and his life was now.

She came back to now, up through levels of consciousness, forgetting where she was, then remembering. His head dipped below her chin, covering her neck and breasts with long, lingering kisses. She sighed with him, her hands roaming.

"Tired?" he whispered.

She hummed, neither yes nor no, simply content to be present and let him do what he wanted.

"I'm so hard for you," he said softly.

She reached down, closed him up in her hand, and desire settled thickly in her chest, along with the damp ache of wanting to feel him in her again. Again, again, she wanted to make love all night with him.

She rolled and put her back to his chest, snugging her butt up into his lap, guiding him into her. "Slow," she said. "Put it in me slow."

Inch by inch he took her, her hipbones snugged in his palms. He wrapped his arms around her waist and groaned into her hair, "God you make me crazy."

She was beside herself with pure, primal want. He rolled up on his knees, bringing her with him. She reached and flung her arms around his neck, loving the feel of him against her back, he was so strong. They kissed deep, mouths soft, slippery and reckless. His hand slid down between her legs. He ran his lips over her back, whispered to her, encouraged and cajoled her, bringing her around.

"I love making you come," he said against her skin. "Want to get in you so deep and fill you up ..."

Her back arched as an explosion rocked her pelvis, made all the feeling leave her hands and feet, made every cell in her body detonate with blue and white feathered shivers, and reduced the entire universe to nothing more than two pleading, primitive words.

Fuck. Me.

He took her by the hips, held her hard, held her open and gave it to her, fucked her, gave it to her good. Until together they went sprawling into the sheets, gasping, coming and clinging to each other.

She cried a little afterward. She couldn't help it.

"Nothing to see here," she said, trying to hide her face but he wouldn't let her. So unbearably sweet, he held her head and kissed the wet trails on her face.

"It's all right," he said, before he enveloped her in his arms and pulled her against his chest. She could feel his heart pounding against hers.

He lay on his back and she lay on him, fingertips playing in his chest hair. A remake of Bob Dylan's "Lay, Lady, Lay" played from the speaker of her phone.

"You think we'll be all right on Monday?" he asked.

"I think so," she said. "I won't pretend nothing will change because of this." She put her chin on her crossed forearms, expression mischievous. "I mean, staff meetings are going to be *slightly* different now that you've seen me naked."

He dragged his fingers through her damp hair, thinking of all the ways he'd seen her tonight, wondering how the hell he was going to compartmentalize all this on Monday.

"It'll be interesting," he said.

It was the best he could do. Really he didn't want to think of it yet.

"Jesus, what time is it?" He instinctively looked at his wrist before remembering his watch was long gone, lost somewhere in the flotsam and jetsam of clothing by the window. He reached to turn the digital clock toward them and she swatted his arm.

"Put that down," she said. "No watching the time."

"You're right." He shoved the clock off the side of the bedside table and turned toward her. He put his hand on the side of her face, played with her hair again, singing softly.

Stay, lady, stay, stay with your man awhile ... Until the break of day, let me see you make him smile.

She turned her mouth into his palm, then nestled into his touch again. Savoring it, storing it, not daring to muse about when, or if she would feel it again.

He asked, "Remember when you said I needed to buy you a drink before I turned forty?"

"Mm."

"I never did."

"Forget it," she said. "Doesn't matter now."

"It doesn't?"

"It wasn't about the drink," she said, and yawned into the back of her hand. "Or about you turning forty. I didn't care if we actually went, I just wanted you to ask."

"Ask?"

"Yeah. Unprompted, without me hinting at it. Of your own spontaneous volition, just ask me one night if I wanted to go grab a beer."

He looked at her a long moment, lifted a finger and pointed at her face. "I'm buying you a damn drink."

She stared back. "You gave me eight orgasms, I don't need the damn drink."

His eyebrows jumped up his forehead. "Eight? Really?"

She shrugged and lay her cheek on her arms. "I lost count ..."

He thought about going for one more, but he was exhausted and the last time, he could tell she was getting sore. Instead he nudged her off him and turned onto his stomach, careening gently into the mattress, utterly spent.

"Lie on my back," he said.

She slid on top of him, tucking the covers around their bodies. Her arms around his arms, her head on his head, her feet on his calves.

"Is this comfortable?"

"It's perfect," he said, weaving her fingers in his. "Can you stay awhile?"

"It's my room, dumbass."

He pulled her embrace closer, wrapped in her arms, in the smell of her perfume and sweat and sex. "I love this," he said softly.

"Me too," she said against his head.

A beat of silence. Then, "Eight?"
She nibbled on his ear. "Ish ..."

She got another when they were in the shower, when he held her hands pinned to the cool tiles and slid into her from behind. Gently, because they were both sore and stinging. But pain shared a blurred boundary with pleasure and the pain of wanting often defeated the pain of excess. And by now, he knew what to do with her.

In the swirling steam, with the hot water cascading down her back, his hands full of soap and full of her breasts, he made her come one last time ...

This time it was her voice that finally turned inside-out and ricocheted off the walls while he threw his head back and made nearly no sound at all.

She texted him, late Sunday night: *Sir?*

She set the phone down and while waiting for a reply, thought about their text message exchanges over the years.

Sir, she always began.

Yes ma'am, he always replied.

When did all the banter start? She remembered that once, they were wrapping up a conversation and she typed, *Beautiful. Thanks.*

He replied, *You're welcome. And you don't need to call me beautiful.*

This was unexpected. She smiled out loud, and without thinking wrote back, *Oh, but I do.*

Not long after, they'd had another exchange: some important file had been due on a Friday, something she needed his time and input to complete. He'd been frustratingly unavailable for days. Repeatedly putting her off—not unkindly, but with a distracted air she found worrisome. She couldn't shake the feeling something was wrong.

Finally at the eleventh hour, she pinged him: *I'm sorry to bother you but we've got to do this now.*

Silence for five minutes, followed by a long block of text:

I'm sorry its been a really really bad day ... An awful week ... I can't even think anymore, I'm sorry ... Please can you just take care of it ... You can do it, you know what to do, work your magic ... I trust you completely. Please, just do this for me.

Startled by this unusual outpouring, she typed back, *Don't give it another thought, I'll take care of it. Go home.*

He replied, *On the train, second beer in ... Don't know what I'd do without you.*

She stared at the screen, stunned. Reached out a fingertip and touched the words *I trust you completely.* They filled up her eyes, caressed something inside her, flooded her with a fierce pride.

I trust you ... Don't know what I'd do without you.

The words felt profoundly intimate. She couldn't have been more pleased if he said he loved her.

In a funny way, he had.

From that day forward, by some unspoken agreement, she began taking things out of his hands. From that point on, she could divine his moods out of his texts. She could read between the lines and know immediately from the words, acronyms or emoticons exactly where his head was. The ability became more honed when they started to gently carry on with each other—not quite flirting, not quite *not* flirting.

She picked her opportunities to engage him carefully. When she pitched him a parting shot, she knew instantly if he had the time or inkling to play with her, or if he couldn't be bothered. She knew a genuine LOL from a polite, disinterested one. All it took was one word typed. Or the lack of a word. The time it took for him to answer her. Or not answer her. And she knew.

Yes ma'am, he typed. ***Are you all right?***

I need a favor, she replied.

A chuckle escaped him. A favor. Sure. After they'd gotten naked, gotten in bed, kissed, touched, licked and explored every square inch of each other. When he could still feel her calf in his back. When his hands still knew the exact shape of her breasts and the jut of her hip bone. When his mouth recalled her taste was somewhere between lemon and basil. When the memory of the feel of her hair spread all across his belly and the heat of her mouth on his cock could still make him stop short and close his eyes. After he slept in her arms. After he let her touch the things he harbored deep in his heart. After he soaped her back and washed her hair. After she put his cufflinks back in and he zipped her dress back up ...

After all that, what the hell was he going to say—no?

He typed back, *Anything* ...

Meet me tomorrow morning, she typed. *I don't want the first time I see you to be at the office. I need to see you outside, walk over with you and ... warm up, I guess.*

Good idea.

Escalator in the Northeast Passage?

OK.

She put the phone down. Picked it up again and started to type, ***You are so my bitch***, but then backspaced it out.

She went back to her book and had read only a couple paragraphs when her phone pinged:

Your bitch will be waiting.

She touched the words with her fingertip.

"This was a good idea," he said.

He was actually surprised how hard it was to look her in the eye without blushing his face off, while a dozen different emotions battled for supremacy in his head. If that head was going into the game, he definitely needed a warm-up.

She fell in step beside him, crisp and sleek in her trench coat. He wished she would take his arm or something. He wanted to touch, but of course that would defeat the entire purpose.

He looked her over with newfound appreciation. She was so wise about these things.

She looked back, an endearing wreath of sleepiness around her eyes, then she tucked a lock of hair behind her ear and knocked her shoulder against his side. "Head in the game, sir?"

"Yes, ma'am."

"See, you've finally bought me a drink," she said as they left Starbucks.

He rolled his eyes and held the door with his back, letting her go first.

They walked up Park Avenue, talked gently about ordinary things, found their footing and sorted themselves out. Arriving at the building together, neither had staked a claim, neither had the upper hand. They got the blushing out of the way, and later ...

... at his regular meeting, he was composed, almost smugly proud of his calm casualness and his ordinary "good morning" as she came in and went to her seat.

She smiled at him with not a degree more or less cordiality than usual, but as she sat down and brushed her hair off her shoulders, her bangles slid from elbow to wrist and back again. The short cascade of chimes made the memory of lovemaking flood his head and make a train wreck of his thoughts. He had to fake a phone call and leave the room, his game face in shambles.

Her fingers were cold and her heartrate ever so slightly elevated, but otherwise she was fine. This was going well. A little surreal, but well. He seemed relaxed too, joking with the managers, sipping his coffee, tapping away on his phone. He got up suddenly and excused himself to take a call.

She smiled to herself. Neither rain nor snow nor sleet nor torrid affair could prevent the usual Monday morning drama.

And then her phone chimed an incoming text. It was him. Her initial pleasure turned to chagrin as she read, *Take those damn bracelets off!*

The heat of memory suffusing her face, she pulled her two silver bangles from her wrist and dropped them in her bag. Right next to the inside zip pocket where she kept one of his collar stays.

He pinged her at the end of the day: *I'm catching a 5:29 train. Walk out with me?*

Packing up now, she replied. *Meet you by the elevator.*

The elevator binged sedately and they glanced at each other.

"Shut up," he mumbled.

"I didn't say anything."

"You thought it."

"You thought it louder."

The doors purred open. He held them with one hand and ushered her in. As she passed, he lightly touched the small of her back.

The doors closed and the floor gave way beneath.

A beat of blushing silence.

"Want to go get a beer?" he said.

Holding his eyes, she reached in her purse, retrieved her bangles and slid them on her wrist. "I thought you'd never ask."

About the Author

A former professional dancer and teacher, Suanne Laqueur went from choreographing music to choreographing words. Her work has been described as therapy fiction, emotionally intelligent romance and contemporary train wreck.

Laqueur's novel *An Exaltation of Larks* was the Grand Prize winner in the 2017 Writer's Digest Awards and won first place in the 2019 North Street Book Prize. Her debut novel *The Man I Love* won a gold medal in the 2015 Readers' Favorite Book Awards and was named Best Debut in the Feathered Quill Book Awards. Her follow-up novel, *Give Me Your Answer True*, was also a gold medal winner at the 2016 RFBA.

Laqueur graduated from Alfred University with a double major in dance and theater. She taught at the Carol Bierman School of Ballet Arts in Croton-on-Hudson for ten years. An avid reader, cook and gardener, she started her blog EatsReadsThinks in 2010.

Suanne lives in Westchester County, New York with her husband and two children.

Visit her at suannelaqueurwrites.com
All feels welcome. And she always has coffee.

Also by
Suanne
Laqueur

THE FISH TALES
The Man I Love
Give Me Your Answer True
Here to Stay
The Ones That Got Away

VENERY
An Exaltation of Larks
A Charm of Finches
A Scarcity of Condors
The Voyages of Trueblood Cay
Tales from Cushman Row
A Plump of Woodcocks

SHORT STORIES
Love & Bravery
An Evening at the Hotel

GIVEAWAY

Enter to win a signed copy of
An Exaltation of Larks
All entrants receive a free ebook of
The Man I Love
http://lqrwrites.com/freebook